The William Shakespeare

CHILDREN'S COLLECTION

Dados Internacionais de Catalogação na Publicação (CIP) de acordo com ISBD

S5271h Shakespeare, William
Hamlet / William Shakespeare. - Jandira, SP : W. Books, 2025.
104 p. ; 12,80cm x 19,80cm. - (Classics).

ISBN: 978-65-5294-200-5

1. Literatura inglesa. 2. Clássicos. 3. Aventura. 4. Fantasia. 5. Imaginação.
I. Título. II. Série.

2025-2513 CDD 823
CDU 821.111

Elaborada por Lucio Feitosa - CRB-8/8803
Índice para catálogo sistemático:
1. Literatura inglesa 823
2. Literatura inglesa 821.111

Text based on the original play by William Shakespeare,
adapted by Georgina Brown
Cover Illustrations by Rishabh Goswami
Internal Illustrations by Adrián Jiménez

1st edition in 2025
www.cirandacultural.com.br

EASY CLASSICS

William Shakespeare

Hamlet

W. Books

Hamlet

The Prince of Denmark.
Stepson and nephew
to Claudius

Claudius

Hamlet's uncle and the
new King of Denmark.
Married to Hamlet's mother

Polonius

A councillor
to Claudius

Ophelia and Laertes

Daughter and son
of Polonius

Gertrude
Queen of Denmark and Hamlet's mother

The Ghost
Seen at night on the castle battlements

Horatio
Hamlet's trusted friend

Rosencrantz and Guildenstern
Hamlet's old friends

Chapter One

At the top of Elsinore Castle in Denmark, Fransisco, a night watchman paced back and forth along the battlements while he waited for his replacement. Every bone in his weary body ached and he shivered in the cold night air. Everything was still and silent, but not peaceful. Fransisco was restless; he nervously gazed into

battlements
A low wall around the top of a castle with rectangular gaps in it for people to shoot things through, such as arrows.

the endless darkness below. He thought about the recent rumours of ghostly sightings and the hairs on the back of his neck began to stand on end. A sudden creak from behind startled him and he froze to the spot in momentary fright.

'Who's there?' he called, forcing his body to turn and face the noise.

'Long live the king!' a familiar voice answered. It was Barnardo, his replacement, right on time. As the clock struck twelve, the two men bid each other goodnight and Barnardo took his place on the battlements. A few moments later, two other men joined him.

'Welcome Marcellus and Horatio. What brings you here tonight?' Barnardo asked.

'Has the ghost appeared tonight? Horatio says it is our imagination,' Marcellus said. 'I've asked him to come tonight so he can see it for himself.'

Horatio shook his head. He did not believe the sightings were real.

'Barnardo, tell him what you saw,' said Marcellus.

'It was last night, when the bell rang to mark one o'clock, Marcellus and I–' he stopped, eyes widening in shock. Before them, glowing faintly and floating just above the stonework of the castle, was the figure of a man. Horatio, Marcellus and Barnardo stood paralysed in shock.

'It looks exactly like the late king,' Barnardo managed to whisper to the other two.

'Speak to it, Horatio,' Marcellus murmured, quietly.

The ghost did not move.

'Who are you? I order you to speak,' said Horatio, his voice trembling slightly.

Then, as quickly as it arrived, the ghost vanished. Horatio stared

at the spot where the spectre had been. 'It wore the same armour as the dead King Hamlet,' he said, his eyes still wide with disbelief. 'I fear this is a bad omen, a sign that something terrible will happen.'

Horatio turned to leave, thinking that he should tell Prince Hamlet what they had seen. Then the ghost appeared again. This time, its arms were held wide open.

'Please. Speak to us. Tell us if you know of any danger,' Horatio pleaded.

Slowly, the ghost moved closer. The men held their breath and waited. In the distance, a rooster crowed and the glowing figure vanished. The men looked at each other unsure of what to do. 'We need Prince Hamlet. If the ghost will speak to anyone, it will certainly be him,' Horatio declared.

Chapter Two

In the castle, the new King of Denmark was speaking to a gathered audience in the throne room. King Claudius spoke in a loud, clear voice. 'Although my brother's death still saddens my heart, the country must move on,' he said. 'I have a new wife, my beloved brother's widow, Gertrude, and together we must address the chaos this country faces.'

As the audience left, he turned his attention to Prince Hamlet,

who was sitting alone in a corner of the throne room. 'What is wrong?' Claudius asked. 'You are the next in line for the throne. I love you like a son and wish for you to be happy here.' His warm voice hid what he truly felt for his nephew. Hamlet kept his eyes on the floor as his mother approached.

'Look up from the ground,' she

said. 'Address the king as a friend.'

Hamlet shook his head. He did not trust his uncle and did not respect him as the new king. No one could ever replace his father. He glanced at Claudius and smiled as best he could. When his mother and the new king left, Hamlet was alone.

'How dull life seems now,' he said to himself. 'My father has only been dead for two months and already my mother has married my uncle. My heart breaks in silence and they wonder why I am mourning,' Hamlet sighed.

Hearing footsteps, Hamlet turned and watched as Horatio and the watchmen entered, cautiously looking behind them.

'Hello, my lord, we have much to tell you,' Horatio said in a hushed voice. Hamlet waved for them to come closer.

'It is about your father. I believe we saw him last night,' Horatio said. Hamlet's face was an odd

mourning

The feeling and expression of great sadness that follows a death or loss.

expression of confusion and hope.

'Let me explain,' Horatio said. 'For the last two nights, these

watchmen have seen a ghostly figure who looks just like your father. On both occasions, they were too afraid to speak.' He paused. 'Last night, I joined them and the ghost appeared – just as they described. I knew your father well and this phantom was identical.'

Hamlet was stunned. 'Are you sure it was him?' he asked and Horatio nodded. For a moment,

Hamlet was too shocked to speak. Eventually he said: 'Let me come with you tonight, if my father's soul is not at peace, I must ask him why and do all I can to help him.'

By the sea, a young woman called Ophelia was saying farewell to her brother, Laertes. He was boarding a ship and returning to Paris to study.

Laertes looked fondly at his sister. 'Be careful of Hamlet,' he warned. 'He may say that he loves you, but his mind is preoccupied with the death of his father. I am

worried he will not treat you as well as you deserve.'

Ophelia laughed at her older brother. 'If you were really worried about me,' she said, 'you would stay here in Denmark instead of returning to France.'

They both watched as their father approached.

'Don't keep your ship waiting,' said Polonius, shaking his son's hand. 'And remember, you will always have a home in Denmark.' Before Laertes could board

the ship, Polonius continued to fuss and give his son advice. 'Remember to do us proud. Keep your friends close, listen to people, don't borrow or lend money and to thine own self be true,' he finally finished, smiling at his son.

Ophelia and her father waved to Laertes as the ship departed. 'What were you discussing before I arrived?' Polonius asked.

'He said to be careful of Hamlet,' she smiled.

Polonius didn't smile. 'Well,

I agree. The prince is trouble. Don't trust his words and ask him to stay away. I don't want you spending any more time with him,' he said sincerely.

Ophelia hid her disappointment. 'Okay, Father,' she agreed.

Chapter Three

High on the castle battlements, in the bitter wind, Hamlet waited with Horatio and the watchmen. Trumpets blared and cannons fired.

'What does that mean?' Horatio asked.

'They sound the trumpets each time the king has a party,' Hamlet said. 'He stays up celebrating and dancing. Other countries laugh at us, but he says it's a Danish tradition. I think it ruins our reputation.' He looked at Horatio and saw that his eyes were wide and fixed on something behind him. Hamlet turned and there was the ghost.

The ghost shone with a pale light, its eyes were empty, but Hamlet knew at once that it was his father. He tried desperately to hold back his tears.

'Father! Why are you here? What is it you want to tell us?' he asked. The ghost motioned for him to follow.

'It wants to get you alone,' said Horatio. 'Don't go, it could be dangerous!'

Hamlet ignored him and said, 'He is the ghost of my father. It is clear he will not speak here, so I must go with him.'

Horatio waited until Hamlet had moved a little further along the battlements before turning to the watchmen. 'We must follow,' Horatio said, 'but not too closely.'

After following the ghost for some distance, Hamlet stopped. 'Where are you leading me, spirit? Father? Speak to me,' he said.

'Listen to me,' the ghost responded in a hollow voice. 'I don't have much time before I must return to pay for my sins. You must avenge my murder!'

'Your murder?' Hamlet said, deeply shocked.

'I was poisoned, in my sleep. The poisoner now wears my crown instead of me!'

'My uncle?' Hamlet asked.

The ghost's head bowed.

avenge

To punish the person responsible for something bad done to you or your family or friends.

'He poisoned me before I could repent my sins and now, I suffer for eternity. Get revenge, but do not harm your mother, leave her fate for God to decide. Remember me,' the ghost pleaded as it faded away. Hamlet stood with outstretched arms.

'Oh, what should I do?' muttered Hamlet. 'My uncle is a murderer and I must set things right!'

Hamlet dropped to the floor, Horatio and the watchmen ran over to him.

repent

To be very sorry for something bad you have done in the past and wish that you had not done it.

'My Lord!' Horatio cried.

The men gently helped Hamlet to his feet.

'I cannot tell you what was said,' Hamlet whispered. 'Swear on my sword that you'll tell no one about what has happened this night.'

The men agreed as Hamlet ran back inside the castle.

The following morning, Ophelia was walking in the castle grounds. Despite her father's and her brother's warnings, she was desperate to see Hamlet again. She wished she could help him to grieve for his father, but lately, he had been so distant.

Ophelia was so lost in her thoughts that she almost didn't see Hamlet, who was pacing back and forth near a fountain. Overjoyed, she rushed over to him. 'My lord! Where have you been?'

Hamlet glanced at her, but continued to pace, muttering to himself. 'Must help Father, must defeat the king,' he said.

Ophelia frowned. 'Are you all right, Hamlet?' she asked, gently placing a hand on his arm.

Hamlet flinched away from Ophelia's hand and glared at her. 'I have no time for this,' he said, dismissively. 'Leave me alone!'

Ophelia did not know what to do. She looked into the face of the man she thought she loved and was surprised at what she saw. His eyes looked wild, his features were twisted and it frightened her. She ran away, leaving Hamlet to stalk restlessly around the grounds once more.

Meanwhile, in another part of the castle, Polonius was thinking about his son. It had been many days since he had set sail for France and he had not received

word that Laertes was safe and sound. He decided to ask Ophelia if she knew anything, but as Polonius opened the door to her chamber, he saw Ophelia sobbing on her bed.

'What has happened, my child?' Polonius asked.

Remembering that her father

had told her to stay away from Hamlet, Ophelia swallowed nervously, then began to tell her father what had happened.

Chapter Four

Concern for Hamlet's behaviour was spreading. When he was not hiding away in his chambers, he was seen wandering aimlessly through the corridors, mumbling to himself.

Claudius was worried. He knew that Hamlet did not like him, but could Hamlet have discovered his murderous secret? He needed to know more, so he summoned two of Hamlet's oldest friends for help.

Rosencrantz and Guildenstern entered the throne room and were welcomed warmly by Claudius and Gertrude.

'We are so pleased you came,' said Claudius. 'If Hamlet is going to speak with anyone, it will be his best friends. See if you can discover what is worrying him so we can work out how to help.'

Rosencrantz and Guildenstern promised they would try their best.

As they left to find Hamlet, Polonius entered, his face red.

‘Your Majesty,’ Polonius said, bowing to King Claudius. ‘I have come to speak to you about Prince Hamlet.’

Claudius leant forward, eager to hear anything about the young prince.

‘I believe I know why he is acting so strangely,’ said Polonius.

Claudius’s heart began to beat faster. *Could Polonius know that he poisoned the old king?*

‘Tell us what you think you know,’ said Claudius.

‘He is in love with my daughter!’ Polonius said, and Claudius

breathed a quiet sigh of relief. 'But now he has cast her aside. I demand to know how he will be punished for his rude behaviour.'

'Gentlemen. What are you doing back in this prison?' Hamlet laughed, taking the hands of Rosencrantz and Guildenstern and shaking them forcefully.

'Prison?' Rosencrantz asked, in confusion.

'Denmark. Don't you think? To me it's a prison,' Hamlet said.

Rosencrantz and Guildenstern exchanged worried looks.

'We've come here for you,' Rosencrantz said, brightly. 'We wanted to see you and we have a surprise that might lift your spirits. We met the actors you used to love to watch and we have asked them to come and perform for us. Just like the old days.'

Hamlet was suspicious about why his old friends had suddenly arrived out of the blue.

out of the blue

If something happens out of the blue, it is completely unexpected.

'Were you sent by my mother and the king?' he asked.

Rosencrantz began to shake his head in denial, but Guildenstern could not lie to his friend.

'Yes, we were sent for,' Guildenstern admitted. 'But we came for *you*. Not them. Trust us, old friend, we only want to help.'

Hamlet looked at them and smiled, his shoulders relaxing for the first time since he had seen the ghost of his father on the battlements.

'When do the actors arrive?' he asked with a small smile.

Chapter Five

To everyone's surprise, including his own, Hamlet enjoyed seeing the actors again and greeted them like old friends. He remembered a play they had once performed at Elsinore Castle when he had been younger. 'It was from a Greek myth where a young warrior called Pyrrhus attacked and killed the old King of Troy to gain power for himself,' Hamlet recalled.

The actors remembered the play and agreed it would be wonderful to perform it again for the new King of Denmark.

'I've heard that people can be moved by actors, so much so that those with guilty consciences often confess when they see a performance that reflects their crimes,' Hamlet said to himself. 'I'll watch my uncle's expressions; if he reacts I'll know he truly did murder my father!'

As he watched the rehearsals, Hamlet started to feel even more pleased with his plan. Soon, he raised his hand for the actors to stop. 'I have a few lines I'd like to add to the play tomorrow. If that is all right with you all?'

he asked. The actors agreed and the rehearsal started again.

The following day, Claudius was keen to see Rosencrantz and Guildenstern and question them about Hamlet's behaviour.

'He seemed happy to see us, but avoids our questions when we ask about his feelings,' Rosencrantz reported.

'Though he enjoys watching

the actors rehearse their play. He's asked that you and the queen attend the performance tonight,' Guildenstern added.

Gertrude and Claudius agreed they would go to the play. After Rosencrantz and Guildenstern had left, Claudius summoned Polonius and Ophelia. 'I have been thinking about what you told me yesterday,' he said. 'But I am afraid I need proof of Hamlet's cruelty to your daughter before I punish him. I have asked Hamlet to come to the throne room. We shall hide and see how he behaves when he finds himself alone with Ophelia.'

Although Polonius was wary of the plan, Claudius was determined. He hoped it was Ophelia's beauty that was causing Hamlet's odd behaviour, and not that he suspected Claudius of murder.

Polonius gave his daughter a prayer book and told her to sit and read until Hamlet arrived. Polonius, Claudius and Gertrude moved to their hiding places.

Walking into the throne room, Hamlet appeared to be speaking to himself. 'To be, or not to be, that is the question – can I live with this pain or is it easier to end it and fall into an endless sleep?'

When Hamlet spotted Ophelia, he seemed to snap out of his daydream. 'Beautiful Ophelia, please forgive me for how I spoke to you last,' he said. 'My mind has been troubled lately.'

Ophelia looked up from her book and greeted him. 'How have you been Hamlet?' she asked. When Hamlet did not answer, she reached into her pocket and pulled out a bundle of letters. 'I want you to take these back; they no longer give me joy,' she said, casting her eyes to the floor.

Hamlet stared at the letters he had written to Ophelia when they had first met. Their declarations of love seemed so innocent. It was a time before his mind had been clouded with grief and thoughts of revenge. 'Everything's a trick,' he said, turning the letters over in his shaking hands. 'Beauty, purity, honesty. No one can escape the sins that have invaded this castle. You should escape. Go to a convent! Save yourself!' With that, Hamlet left the room, muttering to himself.

'Oh heavens, make him sane again,' Ophelia whispered to herself. 'I can't bear to see him like this.'

Hamlet's words had unsettled Claudius. Could he really know the truth about King Hamlet's death? 'My stepson is clearly

convent

A building or group of buildings in which nuns (religious women) live or worship.

muddled,' declared Claudius. 'I shall send him to England on a royal trip. Hopefully, time at sea will help him to collect his thoughts.'

Chapter Six

There was a general buzz of excitement as the actors readied themselves for their performance. Hamlet gave some final instructions to the lead actor: ‘Please deliver the new speech clearly. Don’t make it into a pantomime. No jumping around, waving your arms or shouting,’ he said. The actor nodded in agreement.

Hamlet spotted Horatio in

the audience and went to speak with him.

'Horatio, my friend. You have been kind and patient,' Hamlet began. 'No matter what I've

asked of you, you have done it with positivity and loyalty. Therefore, I'm trusting you with this.' Hamlet leant closer. 'This play has a scene, exactly as my father's ghost described his own murder. Watch my uncle

carefully and note his reactions. We'll talk afterwards. Quick, here they come!'

King Claudius and Queen Gertrude entered the hall where the play was to be performed. Hamlet watched them closely. His mother gestured for him to sit with her, but instead, he sat next to Ophelia and the play began.

When the play reached the scene that Hamlet had told Horatio about, it showed a king being poisoned and his crown taken from him.

On stage, the actor performed

the line that Hamlet had asked for: 'Poison ready, evil thoughts swirling, the darkness of the night protecting me, all show that

the time has come. These magic properties will take his life!' Then he pretended to pour the mixture into the sleeping king's ear.

Unexpectedly, Claudius suddenly stood up. Hamlet caught Horatio's eye, and he nodded.

'Turn on the lights!' Claudius demanded. 'I'm leaving!' and he marched out of the hall.

Hamlet watched him go.

He saw his mother whispering to Polonius, who then came over and told Hamlet that the king was very upset, and his mother wanted to speak to him. Hamlet breathed deeply, hoping that he would be able to keep calm.

Claudius called Rosencrantz and Guildenstern to his private chambers. His desperation was growing. 'We cannot let Prince Hamlet's madness continue. The play tonight clearly shows he is not in his right mind. I'm sending

you both to England with Hamlet. It is your duty to Denmark to watch over him,' he said.

'It's our duty to protect our people and you, Your Majesty,' Rosencrantz answered, obediently. 'And as Hamlet's friends, we will do our best for him.'

When Rosencrantz and Guildenstern left, Claudius fell to his knees. 'I do not know how much more I can take.

My brother's death weighs on me. What prayer could I possibly say to get forgiveness for such an act? My soul's trapped in sin!' he sobbed.

Gertrude waited in her rooms for Hamlet to arrive. Refusing to leave the queen alone, Polonius had hidden behind a tapestry, just out of sight. Hamlet entered the room and bowed to his mother.

'Hamlet, you have offended your father, the king,' Gertrude said.

He looked at her in disbelief. 'You are the queen, your husband's brother's wife and of course my mother, but you must see what you've done!' he replied, angrily. 'You have betrayed the memory of my father!'

'Why do you have that strange look in your eyes?' Gertrude asked, nervously. 'I am worried about you, but I also feel afraid of what you might do.'

At that moment, Polonius reached for his sword, ready to fight Hamlet if Gertrude looked in danger.

Hamlet spun around. 'What was that?' he asked, looking at the tapestry. 'A rat? Or a spy?' he stabbed his sword through the cloth, striking Polonius in the chest.

Gertrude screamed in horror as Polonius fell from behind the tapestry.

Hamlet stepped back, not quite believing his eyes.

Leaving Polonius on the floor, he turned to his terrified mother. It was time to ask her the questions he had been keeping inside for too long.

Chapter Seven

Stunned, Gertrude barely heard as Hamlet questioned her. Why did she marry Claudius so soon after King Hamlet's death? Could she not see he was a villain and a murderer?

His words cut into her and she begged him to stop, covering her ears to block out his words – then suddenly he fell silent. She watched as Hamlet's transfixed

transfixed
To be very still and concentrate on something in wonder, terror or amazement.

gaze followed something she could not see around the room.

Hamlet stared at the ghost of his father. 'Have you come to scold me for not following your command, yet?' he asked, impatiently. He glanced at his mother, who was looking around the room, confused.

'Can't you see him?' Hamlet asked. Gertrude shook her head.

'You're talking to thin air. Your mind is making you see visions,' she said, carefully.

'Protect her,' whispered the ghost and then it vanished once more.

Hamlet shook himself free of the vision and looked at the devastation he had caused in his mother's rooms.

He told his mother not to say a word of what had happened and he hurriedly left.

Moments later, Gertrude found Claudius. Her voice trembled as she told him what Hamlet had done. Claudius sent Rosencrantz and Guildenstern to find and bring Hamlet before him. He smiled, wickedly to himself. 'Now that Hamlet has killed Polonius,' he said to himself. 'It will be easy to convince the whole of Denmark that he has a troubled mind – no one will believe him now. My secret is safe.'

Rosencrantz and Guildenstern found Hamlet looking flustered and alone in the palace gardens.

'My friend, we know what you have done to Polonius,' said

Rosencrantz. 'The king has instructed us to bring you to him.'

Hamlet began walking away. 'Don't believe him. He uses you!' he cried. 'Polonius is with the real

King of Denmark now.'

Rosencrantz and Guildenstern exchanged worried glances before taking Hamlet by the arms. 'We are worried about you,' Guildenstern

said. 'Come with us, we are certain the king only wants to help you.'

Although Hamlet struggled, Rosencrantz and Guildenstern were able to deliver him to King Claudius.

'Hamlet, for your own safety I must send you away,' Claudius said with false concern. 'The ship is ready to take you to England.'

Hamlet was marched out of the room by Rosencrantz and Guildenstern.

Alone, Claudius let out a long breath. 'Oh, England, if you still respect the strength of Denmark, listen to my letters and get rid of Hamlet. Rid me of this pain,' he said.

Chapter Eight

Ophelia wandered through the castle in a trance. When she had heard the news that Hamlet – who she had thought she loved – had killed her father, she fell to the ground in despair. Her world seemed to be crumbling around her. She drifted around the grounds in a daze, talking to herself and crying. She was desperate to see the queen.

Although Gertrude felt guilty

over Polonius's death, she agreed to see Ophelia, and summoned her to the throne room.

Ophelia entered slowly, her eyes staring into the distance. The queen watched her, heartbroken. Clearly, she had lost her mind with grief.

Claudius entered, and took one look at Ophelia, who was now gazing out of the window, then to Gertrude, who simply shook her head.

'How long has she been like this?' Claudius asked.

'Since Polonius was killed,' replied Gertrude.

Ophelia walked over to him, now staring intensely.

'I can't stop crying,' she began. 'I've written to my brother, but I don't know what to do,' she sobbed and ran from the room.

Claudius held his head in his hands.

'Poor girl. Grief has poisoned her mind. Laertes will be back in Denmark at any moment, and he is sure to blame me. I feel respons–' Claudius stopped mid-word, hearing a thunderous rumbling.

The doors to the throne room burst open. Laertes marched in with a band of men behind him who were chanting, 'Laertes for king!'

Laertes held up his hand to silence them.

'Gentlemen, please give me a moment to talk,' he said.

'The king did not kill your father,' Gertrude said quickly, correctly guessing why Laertes was there.

'Then who did?' Laertes asked, sternly. 'I am only after my enemies, no one else.'

Laertes moved to the window and watched as his sister wandered aimlessly below, picking flowers and singing to herself. 'She's lost. Her mind has gone. What terrible suffering has caused this?' he asked.

'May the great axe fall on the guilty. Come and sit. Let's talk,' Claudius said, softly.

'And so you see, I am innocent. Hamlet killed your father and plans to kill me,' Claudius explained to Laertes when they were alone. He sighed theatrically. 'It's difficult because his mother and the public love him, but I think I have solved our problems.'

Suddenly, a messenger entered. 'Hamlet is back!' he said.

'How is that possible? He should be in England by now!' said Claudius, enraged.

'I will confront him,' Laertes said angrily, standing up.

'No, wait,' Claudius said. 'When Hamlet knows you have returned, he will be expecting you to come for him. Why not challenge him to a duel instead? His mother and the public will accept his death if he is killed in a duel. We just have

duel

An arranged fight between two people which sometimes involved using weapons.

to make sure we win!'

'I have poisonous snake oil,' Laertes said. 'I'll lace the tip of my sword with that!'

Claudius nodded and said, 'And to make certain, I'll prepare a drink, laced with the same poison.'

At that moment, Gertrude entered, her eyes wet and cheeks red. 'My dear Laertes,' she sobbed. 'It is your sister! She has drowned!'

Laertes was stunned. 'But she was only here a moment ago!' he cried.

'I was worried about her, so I followed her into the gardens.

A maid told me she had gone to the river and there she was!' Gertrude said before collapsing into heaving sobs.

Laertes was now more determined than ever to get revenge on Prince Hamlet.

Chapter Nine

'Hamlet, it is so good to see you back on Danish soil, but however did you manage it?' Horatio asked Hamlet, as they entered the churchyard.

'I knew that Claudius had plotted to kill me when I reached England,' Hamlet explained. 'Rosencrantz and Guildenstern were taking letters to Claudius's friends and they explained the whole plot. I could never trust them again, no matter how much they were tricked by Claudius. Luckily, the captain of the ship was loyal to my father. When I told him what would happen to me when I arrived in England, he turned the ship around at once.'

Horatio and Hamlet then spotted a grave being dug. The gravediggers had a pile of skulls next to them.

'It is sad to think these were once people,' said Hamlet to the gravediggers.

'It is, this one has been in the ground for twenty-something years,' replied one of the gravediggers.

'Who is it?' asked Hamlet.

'It was the late king's jester, Yorick,' said the second gravedigger.

'Alas, poor Yorick. I knew him Horatio. He was my father's jester. He would play piggybacks with me and make me laugh. All that life has come to this ... a skull buried in the dirt.'

At that moment, they heard the sound of a carriage and footsteps. Crouching behind a gravestone, Hamlet watched Claudius, Laertes and his mother enter the graveyard, walking behind a carriage bearing a coffin.

'Who could it be?' Hamlet asked.

Laertes's eyes streamed with tears. 'My poor sister,' he cried.

Hamlet's heart sank. 'Ophelia?' he cried, realising it was Ophelia's grave being dug.

‘What has happened to my Ophelia?’ he demanded.

Filled with rage at the sight of Hamlet, Laertes stepped angrily towards him, but Claudius placed a hand on his shoulder. ‘Remember our plan,’ Claudius whispered, softly.

Laertes stood straight and, with all the calmness he could summon, said: ‘Hamlet, I challenge you to a duel at sunset to avenge the deaths of my father and sister.’

Hamlet waited nervously in the grounds of the castle where his duel with Laertes was going to happen. 'I feel uneasy, Horatio. Laertes and I are fighting for the same thing – we both want revenge for our fathers' deaths and now ...' He paused for a moment. 'Now poor Ophelia is gone. I wish I could explain everything.'

'It is too late for that,' said Horatio.

Laertes, the king and queen had arrived.

Gertrude looked at her son with pleading eyes. 'Please don't fight,' she urged him, but Hamlet ignored her. As far as he was concerned, her loyalties were with King Claudius.

'Gentlemen!' Claudius said, clapping his hands. 'We know why this duel has been called. Whoever takes the first hit will win and justice will be done. Here are your swords.' He carefully handed Laertes the sword with the poisoned tip, then, as he gave Hamlet his sword, he offered him a goblet.

'I know you and I have not seen eye to eye,' Claudius said. 'But I offer you this drink for luck.'

Hamlet sneered at the offer. 'I will take nothing from you,' he said, before drawing his sword in preparation.

The fight began and with each clash of swords, Gertrude shuddered. 'Hamlet, if you will not take a drink for luck, then I will do it for you!' she said, taking the goblet from Claudius's hand and drinking the poisoned liquid.

Before Claudius realised what was happening, Gertrude collapsed to the floor.

'Mother!' Hamlet cried. In his moment of distraction, Laertes struck with the poisoned blade. Hamlet spun round and ran at

Laertes, tackling him, their swords fell to the ground. In the confusion, Hamlet picked up Laertes's sword and, taking his chance, thrust it at Laertes. Now both young men had been struck with the poisoned blade.

'Curse you, Hamlet!' cried Claudius. 'This poison was for your lips, not hers!'

Hamlet let out a cry of rage. Claudius had not only killed his father, but now his mother too. He charged at Claudius and killed him with his sword.

Staggering backwards, his head dizzy from the effects of the poison, Hamlet fell into Horatio's arms. 'Is there anything I can do to help you, my Lord?' he asked.

'Lie me next to Laertes,' he said. Horatio did as he was asked, and Hamlet reached out to take Laertes by the hand.

'We both wished to take revenge

for the deaths of our fathers,' he said. 'Claudius killed mine, and I killed yours. But before I die, can you forgive me?'

Laertes nodded, before closing his eyes.

In the years to come, Horatio would tell the story of young Prince Hamlet, the greatest king Denmark *never* had.

THE ILLUSTRATED COLLECTION

SIR ARTHUR CONAN DOYLE

SHERLOCK HOLMES

Dados Internacionais de Catalogação na Publicação (CIP) de acordo com ISBD

D754t Doyle, Arthur Conan
The red-headed league / Arthur Conan Doyle ; ilustrado por Arianna Bellucci ; adaptado por Stephanie Baudet. - Jandira, SP : Ciranda Cultural, 2023.
120 p. ; il ; 13,20cm x 20,00cm. - (Sherlock Holmes ilustrado).

ISBN: 978-85-380-9621-4

1. Literatura inglesa. 2. Aventura. 3. Detetive. 4. Mistério. 5. Suspense. I. Bellucci, Arianna. II. Baudet, Stephanie. III. Título. IV. Série.

CDD 823.91
2022-0998 CDU 821.111-3

Elaborado por Lucio Feitosa - CRB-8/8803

Índice para catálogo sistemático:
1. Literatura inglesa 823.91
2. Literatura inglesa 821.111-3

Based on the original story from Sir Arthur Conan Doyle, adapted by Stephanie Baudet
Cover designed by Arianna Bellucci and Rhiannon Izard
Illustrations by Arianna Bellucci

1st edition in 2023
www.cirandacultural.com.br